A Christmas Treasury

Three Story Poems for the Holiday Season

Illustrated by Caroline Ewing

A GOLDEN BOOK • NEW YORK

Western Publishing Company, Inc., Racine, Wisconsin 53404

A VERY SMALL CHRISTMAS

I wonder if the chipmunks know
When everything is white with snow
And night starts coming very fast
That Christmastime is here at last?

And do the little chipmunks go
To sleep, quite early, in a row—
With Christmas dreams inside their heads
And extra blankets on their beds?

And do they hop up just at dawn
And put their robes and slippers on

And hurry out to peep and see
If someone brought a Christmas tree?

If someone did, I wonder who?
Their chimney's small to wriggle through!
Their Christmas tree must be a twig—
But maybe chipmunks think it's big.

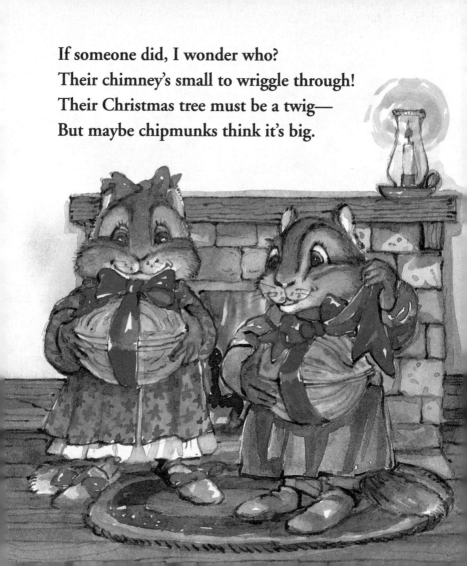

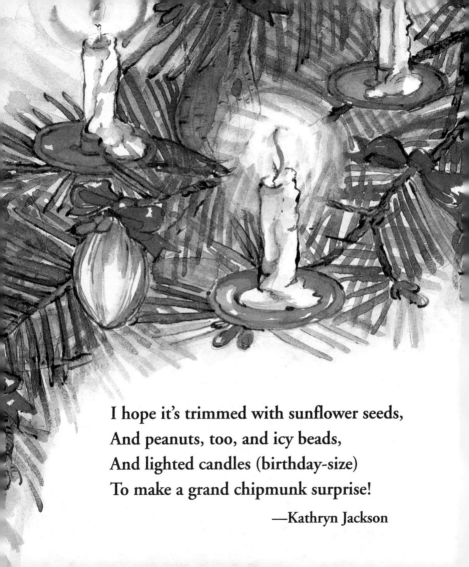

I hope it's trimmed with sunflower seeds,
And peanuts, too, and icy beads,
And lighted candles (birthday-size)
To make a grand chipmunk surprise!

—Kathryn Jackson

A BIRTHDAY GIFT

What can I give him,
Poor as I am?
If I were a shepherd
I would bring a lamb,
If I were a wise man
I would do my part.
Yet what can I give him?
Give my heart.

—Christina Rossetti

MOUSE CHRISTMAS

Oh, the wonderful bits
That folks drop as they go,
Cooking and baking
And hurrying so!

Citron and raisins
And powdery spice,
Sugar and currants—
It's nice to be mice
In this big busy house
With Christmas ahead!

We find tinsel and ribbon
To hide in our bed,
And shavings of chocolate,
And the sugary rind
Of sweet spicy orange.
And sometimes we find . . .

Crisp peppermint chips
All striped red and white,
And gingersnap crumbles—
A wonderful sight!

We'll fill up our stockings
When Christmas Eve comes
With the savory bits
And the wonderful crumbs;
Citron and raisins
And sugar and spice—

Oh, just before Christmas
It's NICE to be mice!

—Kathryn Jackson